"THE GUNN QUEEN"
CREATED BY RICHARD G.MOONEY AND YANKO SUPER

SCRIPT AND STORY: RICHARD G.MOONEY.
ART AND LETTERING: YANKO SUPER.
EDITOR: LELAND BJERG.
GUNN QUEEN LOGO: SILVANO BELTRAMO.
GAELIC TRANSLATION: N. SÚILLEABHÁIN

FIRST EDITION IN ENGLISH: AUGUST 2024.

ISBN: 978-1-7384886-8-1

RGM.SCOT
HTTPS://RGM.SCOT
@RICHARDGMOONEY

@YANKOSUPER_

THE GUNN QUEEN
INTERLOPER

VOLUME 1

STORY:
RICHARD G. MOONEY.

ART:
YANKO SUPER.

MOONWIDD
COMICS

CHAPTER I: SPIRITED AWAY

LONG AGO THE AULD GODS OF THE SUN AND MOON FOUGHT TO CONTROL THE KINGDOM OF HIGHER ALBA AND HER POWERFUL ALLY, THE DOMINION, IN A WAR THAT TORE THESE LANDS ASUNDER.

BOTH ARE HOME TO MAGICAL LUNAR RELICS THAT PROTECT THEM FROM THE FIRES OF THE ALL CONSUMING ENDLESS SUN.

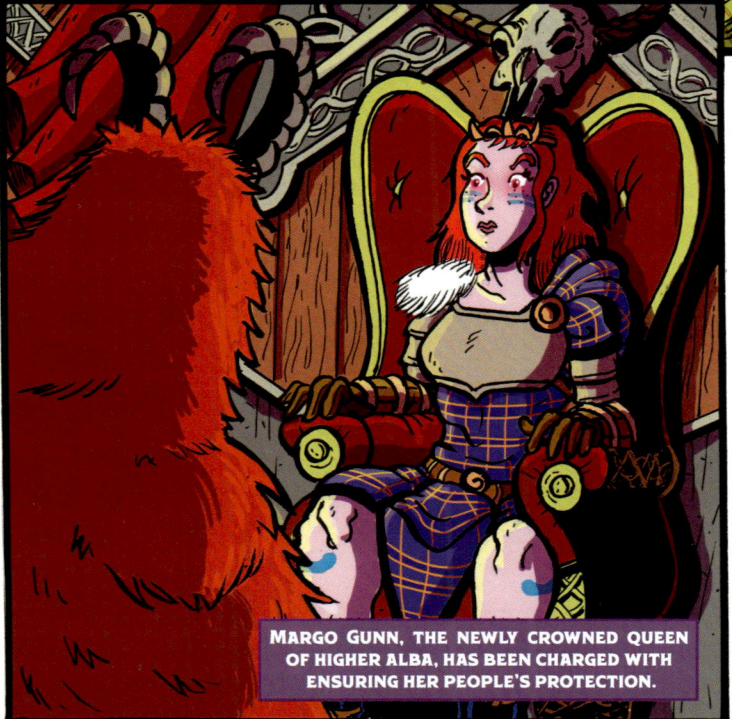

MARGO GUNN, THE NEWLY CROWNED QUEEN OF HIGHER ALBA, HAS BEEN CHARGED WITH ENSURING HER PEOPLE'S PROTECTION.

BORN UNDER A BLOOD MOON 25 WINTERS AGO, MARGO IS A DEMI-GODDESS...

...WITH THE ABILITY TO TURN SOULS INTO PROJECTILES CALLED "SOULLETS".

AND TONIGHT, IN THE WILDS OF HIGHER ALBA...

...THE GUNN QUEEN HAS BEEN SPIRITED AWAY.

NOW...

I KNOW NOT WHO HUNTS US, ONLY THAT THEIR PURSUIT CONTINUES. SHOULD THEY FIND US...

...THEN WE SHALL GREET THEM WITH FIRE AND STEEL.

NEVERTHELESS, ECK, OUR ESCAPE REMAINS A BLUR TO ME.

WE STRUCK AN ACCORD. I AM TO BE YOUR GUARDIAN AND YOU, MY WARD.

THE RESULTING ONSLAUGHT DULLED MY BLADE AND SPENT ALL YOUR ROUNDS.

MANY WERE MAIMED BUT NONE WERE SLAIN.

THANK YOU, NO SOULLETS WERE MADE OR USED. THANK GOODNESS.

I STILL HAVE MY FIRE ROUNDS. TO KNOW NO LIVES WERE TAKEN DOES PROVIDE ME SOME SOLACE.

KRAA

KRA

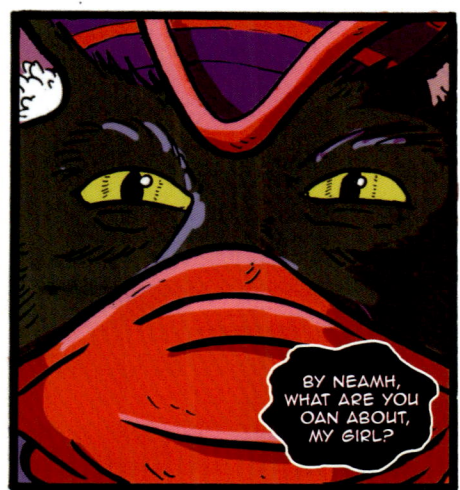

DIE!!!

AS I ALWAYS SAID, LASS...

...YOUR FURY WILL BE YOUR UNDOING.

OUR BUSINESS IS NOT YET FINISHED.

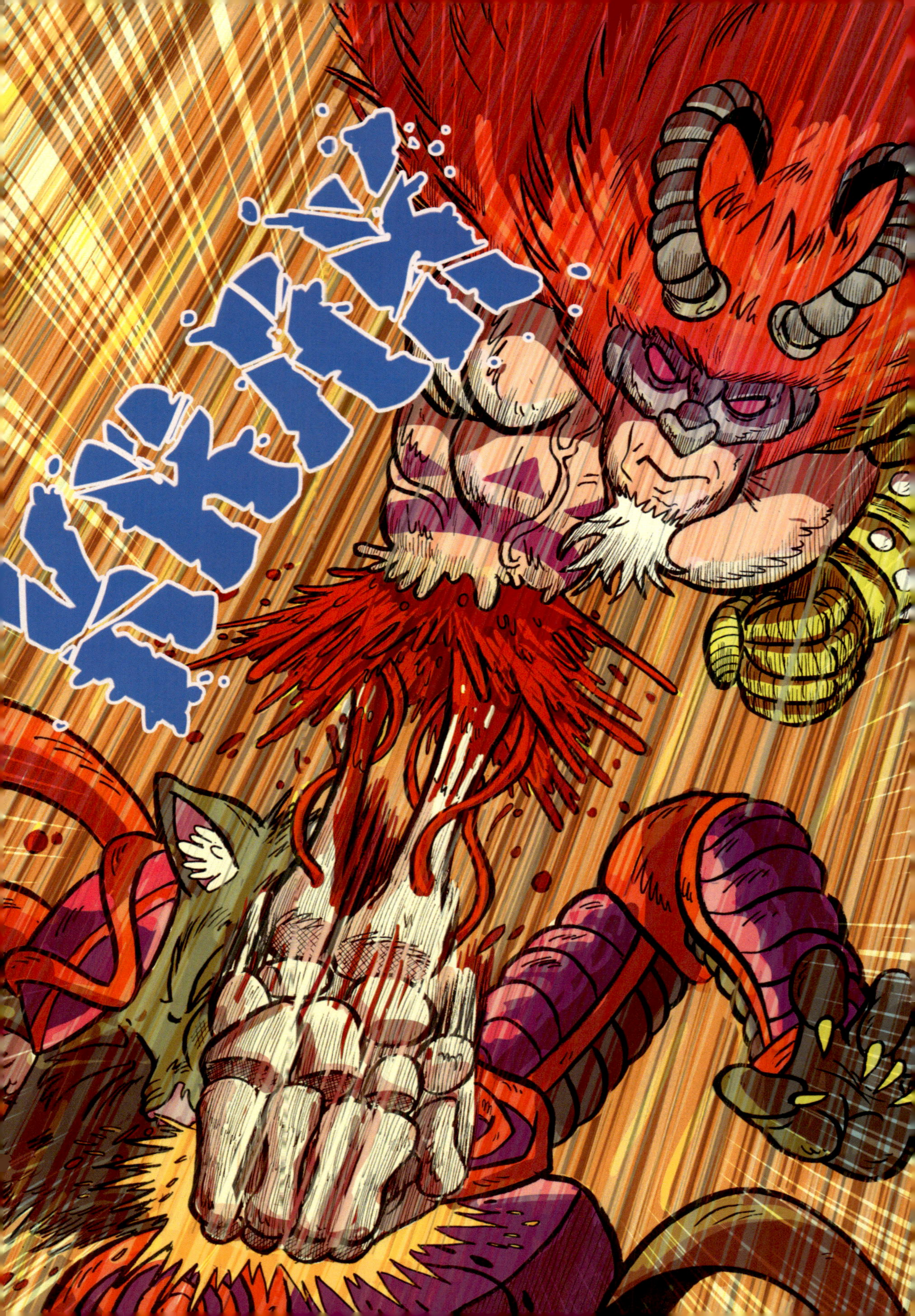

NISEAG!!!

SPLASH

THAK

NEVER RETURN!

THUK

!

CHAPTER 2: THE FALL

SO, YOU'RE A CAT-SITH?

AYE. I NEEDED THE EXTRA STRENGTH FOR THE FIGHT.

TAKE IT EASY HERE.

...THE BAIRN OF THE BLOOD MOON, AS THEIR WARD.

BUT, IF IT GIVES YOU UNGODLY POWERS, WHY NOT JUST BE THE CAT-SITH ALL THE TIME?

IT'S NOT WITHOUT COST.

FOCUS ON FLYING MARGO, RAYTH MIGHT BE YOURS ONE DAY.

OH, YOU HEAR THAT, RAYTH.

KAKAW

BUT SERIOUSLY, WHAT TOLL DOES IT TAKE?

ONE HOUR AS THE FELINE AGES MY MORTAL BODY ONE YEAR

SAVED BY HER MYSTERIOUS MENTOR, NANA, FROM THE SUN DEMON ECK, MARGO RETURNS HOME.

ALLFATHER ALMIGHTY!! HOW MANY TIMES HAVE YOU USED IT?

MORE THAN I SHOULD HAVE.

NOW, TAKE US DOWN.

THERE, SHE'LL NEED TO SET THINGS RIGHT AFTER HURTING HER PEOPLE WHILE UNDER ECK'S SPELL.

BUT AS HISTORY TEACHES US, WHENEVER A MONARCH OPENS FIRE UPON THER KIN, ROYAL LINES TEND TO GET...

WAHEY!!

SWOOOSH

...UNMADE.

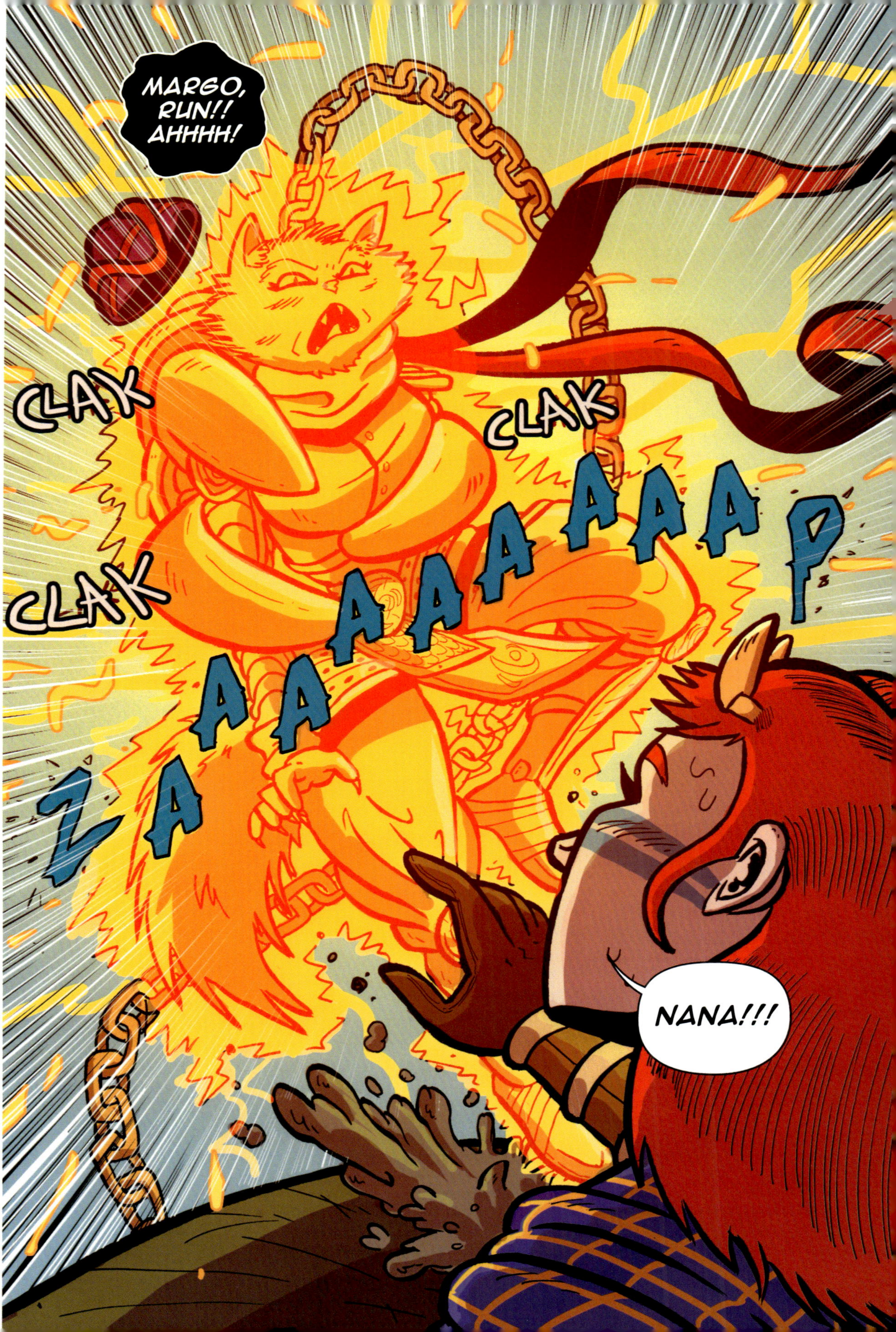
MARGO, RUN!! AHHHH!
CLAK
CLAK
CLAK
ZAAAAAAAAAAP
NANA!!!

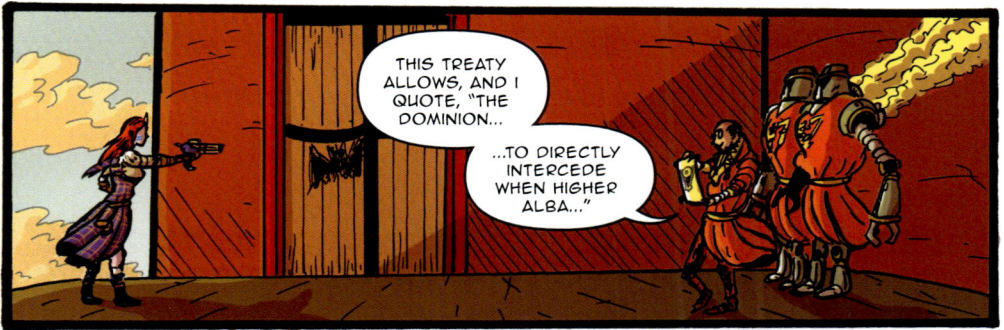

BANG

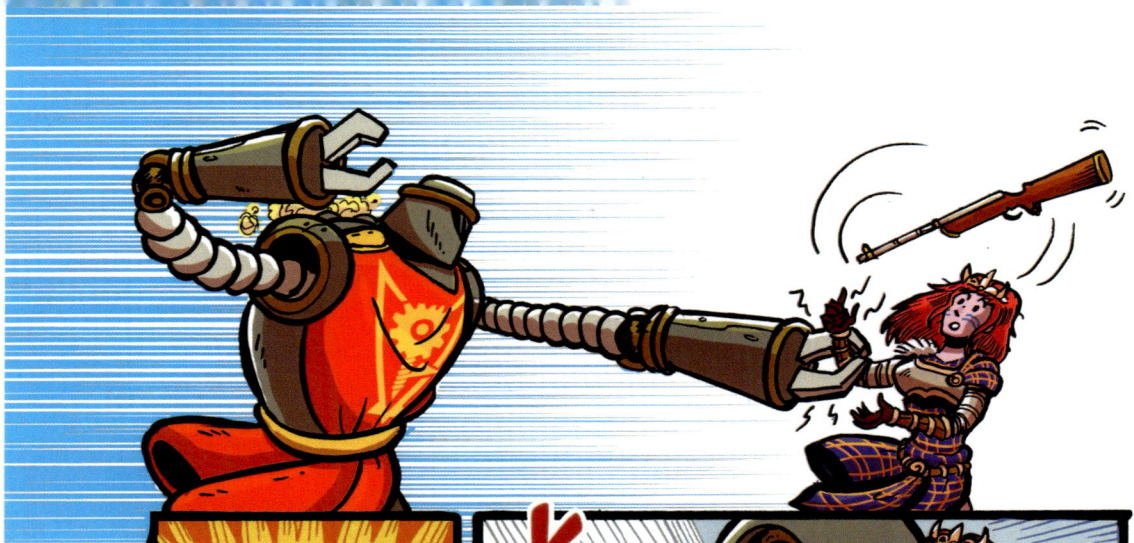

NANA...

CHAPTER 3: BEAST WITHIN

FALLEN QUEEN.

FWEEEE... ...EEEEET

sniff
sniff

purrrrrrrrrr
STOP CREATURE!
HUSH, LASS. MY SALIVA AND PURRS CAN HEAL ALL WOUNDS.
MY INJURIES ARE GONE!

PURRRRRRRRR
THANK YOU, KIND CREATURE. YOU SAVED MY LIFE.
TELL ME, WHERE ARE YOU FROM? WHY SAVE ME?
YOU NEEDED SAVING.
GRANDMA SAYS I WAS BORN IN "THE BEAUTIFUL ISLE", BUT MY EARLIEST MEMORIES ARE OF HERE.
THAT IS A FAR AWAY LAND. DO YOU KNOW HOW OLD ARE YOU?
ABOUT 20 WINTERS.
GOODNESS, YOU'RE STILL GROWING.
THE RECORDS OF WILD ALBA NEVER MENTIONED A LONGMAO.
WHAT'S A LONGMAO?
YOU ARE. IT MEANS CAT DRAGON IN MY TONGUE. DO YOU HAVE A NAME?
GRANDMA CALLS ME JOJIUKI.
NICE TO MEET YOU JOJIUKI. I'M-
-MARGO GUNN, QUEEN OF HIGHER ALBA. PLEASED TO MEET YOU, YOUR MAJESTY.
HOW DO YOU KNOW THAT?
GRANDMA TOLD ME ALL ABOUT YOU.
AND WHO IS "GRANDMA"?
THE ONE YOU CALL "NANA".

LATER.

FAMHAYREN BEAST. GIANT OF THE SKY. THE ENDLESS BLUE CALLS YOU HOME.

YOUR BONES REST EASY. YOUR DUTY FULFILLED.

MAY YOU FLY FREE FOREVER MORE.

DO IT.

FWOOOOOOOSH!!

I NEVER KNEW HIM.

HE WAS A LOYAL BIRD, BRAVE TO THE END.

BANG

NOW, YOU CAN HELP US OR MY FRIEND HERE MIGHT GET HUNGRY.

I'LL NEVER HELP YOU ALBAN SCUM!

NOW I'M GOING TO ASK YOUR GOOD SELF.

WHERE THE HELL ARE ECK AND NANA?

RIGHT HERE.

What are the ingredients that make up Gunn Queen?

Take one of the saddest moments of your life, and add all that you love in life and culture to tell a story that only you could tell. In my case, my Nana died while I was away from home and I couldn't be with her due to circumstances beyond my control. I couldn't see her at the end. So, I wrote her into my book.

The character of Nana embodies her best parts. As in life, she is the 'mentor' in this story, Margo's very own Obi-Wan Kenobi. Margo isn't based on any one person. She is based on all the women in my life but she is her own woman. In this story we meet her at the start of her 'Gunn Queen' journey. She isn't The Gunn Queen yet. This story is about her journey to that destination. How many chapters will that be? We do not know.

She's not a gun Queen, like a queen of guns. Gunn is a name in Scotland. Her weapons are guns, but she's also very efficient at hand-to-hand combat.

Originally, the story was supposed to be a mythological tale incorporating elements of Scottish and Celtic folklore. While it still embodies elements of that original vision, it has gone on to become its own thing.

Originally, this was called The Gunn King and was written as a novel in 2020 and much of what you read now is that story. Why did we change to the Gunn Queen? Honestly, Margo - a character in the novel - was a much better protagonist.

I've worked in newspapers, television, video games, animation and education. But my first love that inspired all that I love was comics. Gunn Queen has been a novel, an animation script, and, finally, now, a comic.

I want to pay special tribute to Gunn Queen cocreator Yanko Super. Without him, none of this happens. He illustrated everything you see here and brought this vision to life over a period of 18 months. He is a special talent and 'one to watch'. Gracias, mi amigo. We're hard at work on the next part.

On top of that, I'd also like to thank my wife, my cat, my mum, dad, sister and wider family. Cheers to all my friends for their support. I believe in Gunn Queen with all my heart. It is the one of the best things I've ever done or made and I am so glad you have decided to buy it. I really appreciate your support.

-Richard G. Mooney

Margo's tartan is a mix of purple and gold. It's so thick and durable it doubles as armour. There's more to this gun than meets the eye. Called Shuurtr, it can fire a variety of magical and elemental rounds, but it has a special central chamber and is more powerful than it looks.

Nana is wearing armour inspired by ancient Chinese folklore. In fact, she wields a Guan Dao, just like Guan Yu, the Chinese God of War. As a Cat-Sith, she gets a major power boost and is able to go toe-to-toe with gods and powerful beings such as Eck. She has guarded Higher Alba for generations. But her power comes at great cost.

Eck's tartan is a mix of red and gold. His sword is called Chib, which in certain parts of Scotland means to stab. See what we did there? Eck is a demigod. He's mean, manipulative, wildly strong and wants Higher Alba for himself. But why? And where does he get all that power from?

Hey! Yanko Here! ... I wanted to use these next pages to show you some of my process as an artist. In this case, I wanted to show you the process of the double splash page in chapter 2... the one I call " Welcome to Higher Alba".

First of all, after reading Rich's script, I do a rough layout (size A5), that I call "storyboard", since it is very similar to the storyboards used in the early development of movies.

Once Richard is satisfied with the sketch, I move onto pencils, which is basically drawing on the page with a graphite pencil (you know, the one you used to use in school), In two A4 sheets of paper.

After that I move to "inks" for which I use two A3 Bristol papers together (yes, the original is basically a A2), and I ink using a brush (a kolinsky size 1)with black ink and some Sakura Pigma Micron Pens (02, 05 and 08).

And finally, I scan this bad boy to start coloring digitally.

Writer/Co-Creator

Richard G Mooney, known as Rich is a Scottish writer who has worked across print, web, TV, animation, and video games. Most recently, he was the Game Writer for the PC game *Volcanoids*. Rich also served as the writer on many videogame and creative projects. He has previously taught academic writing at National Taiwan University. He currently works as an Innovation Journalist for NationalWorld. He lives in Greater Glasgow with his wife and cat.
Visit **https://rgm.scot** for more of his work.

Artist/Co-Creator

Yanko Super is a comic book artist and writer from Chile, where he is known for his authorial works such as *Lupo*, *Zonder* and more. Trained in comic book illustration at Escuela Superior de Dibujo Profesional (ESDIP) in Madrid, Spain, Yanko has been working as a professional artist since 2020. He creates everything by hand: from pencils to inks, and then brings pages to life with eye-popping digital colours and deft lettering. Yanko lives in Valdivia, Chile, with his girlfriend, Carolina, and three cats.